Cara Takes Time

Written by Megan Borgert-Spaniol

Illustrated by Lisa Hunt

GRL Consultants,
Diane Craig and Monica Marx,
Certified Literacy Specialists

Pull
Ahead
READERS
People Smarts

Lerner Publications ◆ Minneapolis

Lerner Publications
An imprint of Lerner Publishing Group, Inc.
241 First Avenue North
Minneapolis, MN 55401 USA

For reading levels and more information, look up this title at www.lernerbooks.com.

Main body text set in Mikado 24/41
Typeface provided by Hannes von Doehren.

The images in this book are used with the permission of: Lisa Hunt

Library of Congress Cataloging-in-Publication Data

Names: Borgert-Spaniol, Megan, 1989- author. | Hunt, Lisa (Lisa Jane), 1973- illustrator.
Title: Cara takes time / Megan Borgert-Spaniol ; Lisa Hunt.
Description: Minneapolis : Lerner Publications, [2023] | Series: I care (Pull ahead readers. People smarts. Fiction) | Includes index. | Audience: Ages 4–7. | Audience: Grades K–1. | Summary: "Cara takes care of herself by making time to walk, listen, rest, and more. Pairs with the nonfiction title, I Care for Myself"— Provided by publisher.
Identifiers: LCCN 2021040277 (print) | LCCN 2021040278 (ebook) | ISBN 9781728457697 (lib. bdg.) | ISBN 9781728461441 (eb pdf)
Subjects: LCSH: Readers (Primary) | LCGFT: Readers (Publications)
Classification: LCC PE1119.2 .B67267 2023 (print) | LCC PE1119.2 (ebook) | DDC 428.6/2—dc23

LC record available at https://lccn.loc.gov/2021040277
LC ebook record available at https://lccn.loc.gov/2021040278

Manufactured in the United States of America
1 – CG – 7/15/22

Table of Contents

Cara Takes Time

Cara takes time to walk.

Cara takes time to listen.

Cara takes time to draw.

Cara takes time to think.

Cara takes time to nap.

Cara takes time for herself.

How do you take care of yourself?

Did You See It?

draw

nap

walk

Index